MW00762944

Disney

PLUTO

DISNEY

PLUTO

Behind the Creation of Mickey's Best Friend

By Eden Greenberg

San Rafael, California

Mickey Mouse is, by far, Walt Disney's most famous character. Created in 1928, Mickey began his career as a silly, mischievous mouse. Mickey's chief goal, it seemed, was to win over the lovable Minnie Mouse. But wooing Minnie was not easy. Mickey's attempts to gain Minnie's affection often landed him in dangerous situations, with no one to count on for help. Mickey needed someone to play off—someone to get into scrapes *with*. He needed a best friend.

Extremely lovable and fiercely loyal, Pluto is Mickey's devoted pet and closest friend. Unlike the other characters in Mickey Mouse's world, Pluto does not walk upright, wear clothing, or talk. He is a dog, through and through. Some of his favorite pastimes include playing catch and going for walks with Mickey. Where Mickey goes, Pluto follows. Of course, therefore, in addition to enjoying the simple pleasures in life, Pluto often finds himself partaking in Mickey's antics—no matter how silly or risky. But, after all, isn't that what a best friend is for?

Although the world knows Pluto as Mickey's faithful pup, the lovable dog actually didn't begin his career that way. When Pluto made his first appearance, he was not a friend to Mickey at all. In fact, he appeared as a nameless bloodhound who must track down an escaped Mickey and return him to prison!

In October 1930, Pluto made his second appearance, this time in the Mickey Mouse short *The Picnic*. He played the role of Minnie's pet, a hound named Rover, who accompanies Mickey and Minnie on a picnic. Although not yet officially in the role of Pluto, the dog displays many of the mischievous traits audiences would later see in Mickey's pal. The hound even goes so far as to chase rabbits and cause damage to Mickey's car. Luckily for Mickey and Minnie, the lovable pup is not all trouble. In fact, he turns out to be quite helpful. When a thunderstorm suddenly breaks out, the hound puts his tail to good use as a windshield wiper for Mickey's car!

On May 3, 1931, Walt Disney released the third Mickey Mouse short to feature Pluto. This short was different from Pluto's previous appearances, as it established his place as Mickey's pet and faithful companion. The short features Mickey and Pluto on a trip to the woods to hunt for moose. Things go awry when Pluto picks up a stick that looks like a set of antlers, and Mickey mistakes him for a moose. Mickey, thinking he has accidentally shot Pluto, is devastated. While Pluto turns out to be fine, the short shows just how much Mickey loves his devoted pup.

Although the 1931 short is technically a Mickey Mouse short, Pluto is the true star. Much of the action follows the playful dog as a series of pests attempt to make a home in his fur and later as he ultimately comes across the much sought-after moose. While this short is the first short to introduce Mickey's dog as Pluto, the fundamentals of his personality are not yet clearly established. In fact, this is the one short in which Pluto speaks, first saying, "Kiss me!" to Mickey and later alerting Mickey to the moose's presence by repeatedly houghing the word "moose."

As Mouse's best friend, Pluto is eager to please Mickey. But there is more to Pluto than just a happy-go-lucky dog. Although rarely outright disobedient, Pluto is a bit of a mischief-maker. He is frequently portrayed with an angel on one shoulder and a devil on the other. These two sides of Pluto's conscience offer the lovable pup advice when he finds himself in a tough situation. Although Pluto tends to listen first to the devil, his good nature usually wins out and he ends up taking the angel's advice.

New Tales from Old Mother Goose
AS TOLD BY WALT DISNEY

Of course, Pluto's goodness does not *always* win out. He has a jealous streak, especially when faced with the idea of Mickey getting another pet. Also, not overly fond of cats to begin with, Pluto has a particular dislike for Minnie's cat, Figaro, whom he views as a rival for Minnie's affection. Pluto is also a bit of a coward and easily frightened, although he will put aside his cowardice without hesitation and display true bravery in order to protect Mickey.

Although Pluto does not intentionally cause trouble, his curiosity often lands him in hot water. Nowhere is this clearer than in a sequence from the 1934 Mickey Mouse short *Playful Pluto*, in which the playful pup tracks a fly across a room only to find himself stuck to a sheet of flypaper. Determined to find a way out of his situation, Pluto tugs at the paper, which moves from his nose to his front paws to his back paws. Throughout the scene, Pluto repeatedly stops to think about the best way to free himself. But unfortunately for the poor pup, the situation escalates until he ends up humorously wound up not only in the flypaper, but also in the window shades.

This sequence is one of the first times where Pluto appears as a major character in a short. It is considered an important scene within Disney history and more broadly in animation history, as it demonstrates Disney animators' ability to use a character's personality to build humor around the simplest of scenarios. More importantly, it was the first time an animated character was seen to think through consequences and have a mind of its own. Disney legend and noted animator Frank Thomas has said of this scene, "This was the key to making a believable character—getting the character to think and puzzle out a situation. Pluto was ideal for this."

Beach Picnic

In fact, this scene is so important to Disney's history that it inspired a similar scene in the 1939 Donald Duck short *The Beach Picnic*. Animated this time in color, Pluto follows an ant who is trying to steal Donald's food across the beach, only to get stuck again on a sheet of flypaper left out by Donald to catch the ants.

Although *The Beach Picnic* was one of the few shorts to primarily feature Donald and Pluto, it wasn't the first. In 1936, the two starred together in *Donald and Pluto*, a short that featured Donald as a plumber attempting to fix leaky pipes. Chaos ensues when Donald's hammer gets stuck to a magnet. In the process of prying the two apart, Donald breaks the pipes, waking Pluto and ultimately pulling his bone away from him. Pluto, who is desperate to get his bone back, accidentally swallows Donald's magnet and ends up with his bone—as well as some forks, knives, and dishes—stuck to him.

Donald and Pluto followed up *The Beach Picnic* with a handful of joint shorts throughout the 1940s. In *Window Cleaners*, Donald is a window washer, with Pluto working as his assistant. Unfortunately for Donald, Pluto gets distracted by a flea, causing Donald to fall from the scaffolding Pluto was hoisting up. In another 1940s short, Pluto is towing Donald in a rowboat when he gets distracted by a frog and loses control of the boat. Disney used Pluto's distractibility frequently in Pluto and Donald shorts, as Donald Duck's notoriously short temper makes an excellent comic foil to Pluto's absentmindedness.

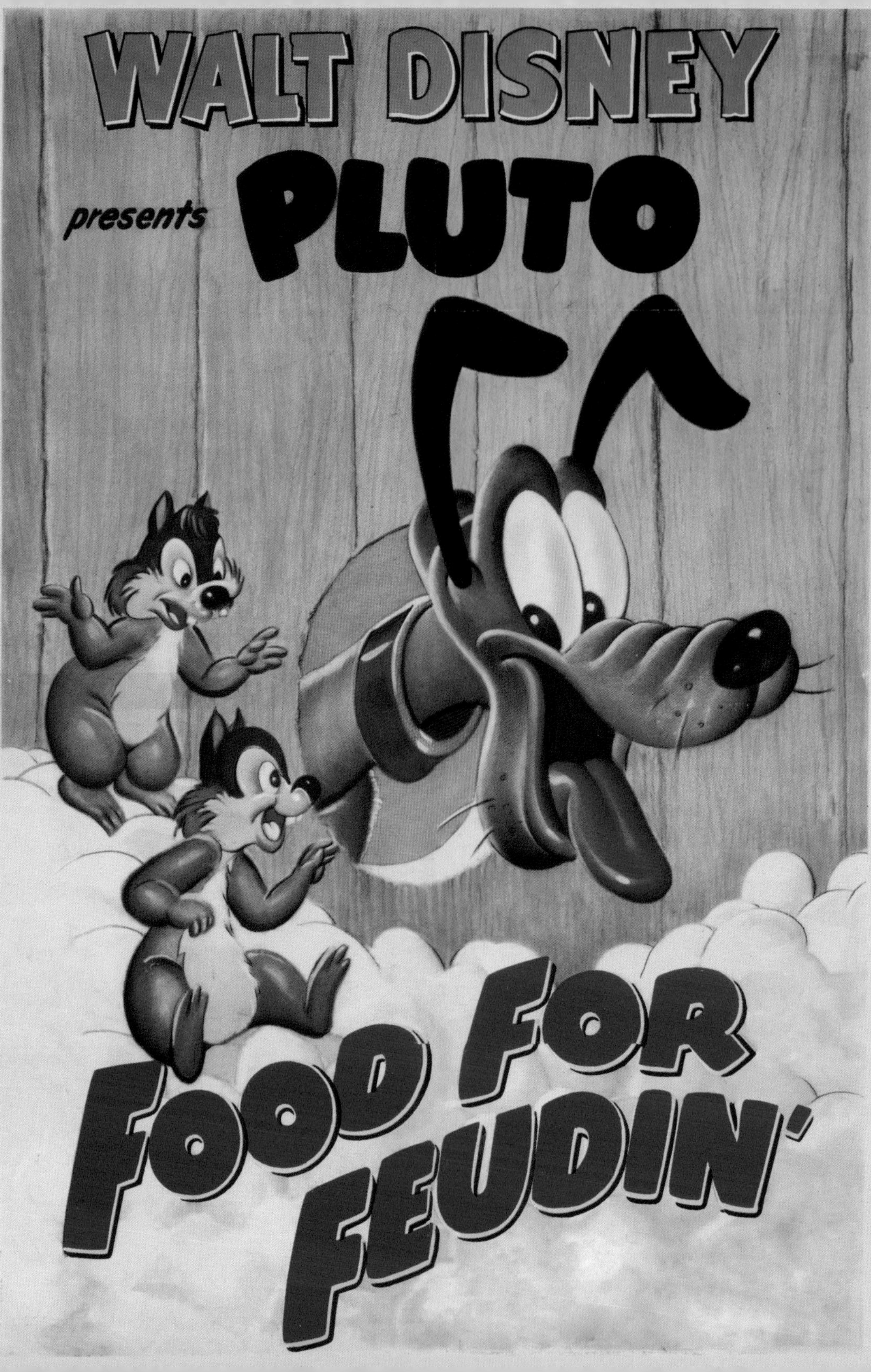
WALT DISNEY
presents
PLUTO
FOOD FOR
FEUDIN'

Donald is not the only character Pluto plays well against. In 1950, Pluto starred against the rascally chipmunks Chip and Dale in *Food for Feudin'*. In the short, Chip and Dale happily fill a tree full of hazelnuts. When Pluto unknowingly buries his bone in the same tree, he starts an avalanche of nuts that spill straight into his doghouse. Chip and Dale quickly hide themselves in a pair of gardening gloves and, tossing a ball back and forth for Pluto, trick the pup into dragging his doghouse all the way to their tree so they can take their nuts back. Although annoyed when he discovers the chipmunks' trick, Pluto eventually gives in to his good nature, laughing along with the merry animals.

Pluto again shared the spotlight with Chip and Dale in 1952's *Pluto's Christmas Tree*. In this memorable holiday classic, Chip and Dale encounter Pluto in the woods and begin to tease him. When Pluto gets angry and comes after them, the two hide in a tree. But their chosen tree is the same one Mickey has decided to chop down for his Christmas tree. The two chipmunks end up as unwitting guests in Mickey's home, where they wreak havoc on his Christmas decorations. Mickey, thinking Pluto has caused the damage, grows angry with his pet, only to discover the true culprits. All ends happily, with Mickey welcoming the chipmunks into his home to celebrate Christmas with him and Pluto.

PLUTO—The Pup

While it's true that Pluto makes a great costar, as seen in his many appearances with Mickey and Donald, he also makes a great solo star. In the early 1930s, Pluto took center stage in two *Silly Symphonies* shorts. The first short, *Just Dogs*, features Pluto breaking out of the pound with the help of another dog. Together, the two free all the other dogs in the pound. The second, *Mother Pluto*, showcases Pluto playing the role of mother to a group of newly hatched chicks whose eggs have happened to hatch in his doghouse.

In 1937, Pluto's star power was at last fully recognized, and he was given his own series of shorts. The series was originally known as *Pluto the Pup* but was shortened simply to *Pluto* in 1940. Over the years, Pluto would star in 48 cartoons of his own, but the first of the shorts, which features Pluto as a father to five pups, remains the most iconic. When the pups' mother, Fifi, goes out to find food, Pluto is left alone to care for his offspring. Unfortunately for Pluto, the pups have even more energy than he does and prove too much for one tired father to wrangle!

Although Pluto usually appears in shorts with Mickey, Minnie, and Donald, he interacts with many other characters. Pluto's love interest and the mother of his quinpuplets, Fifi, is Minnie's dog. Although often jealous of Pluto, at heart Fifi is kind and gentle. She and Pluto appear together in several shorts, including *Society Dog Show*, in which Pluto bravely rescues Fifi from a fire that breaks out during a dog show.

A seductive dachshund named Dinah later replaced Fifi as Pluto's love interest. Dinah made her first appearance in Pluto's world in 1942 in the short *The Sleep Walker.* The pup instantly falls head-over-paws in love with the petite brown dachshund, but his affection is not immediately returned. In fact, the two appeared in several shorts together over the years, each of which focused on Pluto having to win Dinah all over again. Although Pluto's love for Dinah has been unwavering since her first appearance, Dinah's affections are less certain. The little dog has been known to date Pluto's nemesis, Butch, a bulldog who takes great pleasure in antagonizing his foe.

Of course, no matter whom else Pluto might star against, his best costar will always be Mickey Mouse—so it should come as no surprise that, of all the Mickey and friends shorts, the only Oscar win went to Mouse and Mouse's best friend.

In 1941, Walt cast Mickey and Pluto in a short called *Lend a Paw*, in which they rescue a kitten. The short earned high praise and won the 1941 Academy Award for best animated short.

The opening credits for *Lend a Paw* read, "This picture is dedicated to the Tailwagger [sic] Foundation in recognition of its work in lending a paw to man's animal friends." The Tailwaggers Foundation, which funds qualified nonprofit organizations that aid sick animals, returned the love, awarding Pluto the Boscar— its own version of the Academy Award—for most promising dog actor of the year.

Although incredibly well received, *Lend a Paw* was one of the last shorts Mickey and Pluto would star in together. In fact, between 1941 and 1953, the two only appeared in seven Mickey Mouse shorts together. The last of these, *The Simple Things*, features Mickey and Pluto on a fishing trip and contains a humorous sequence in which Pluto gets a clam stuck in his mouth. Pluto rushes to Mickey for help, but Mickey mistakenly thinks the pup is asking him for food. He happily feeds Pluto a hot dog, which the clam enjoys so much that it proceeds to steal Mickey's sandwich and a full pepper shaker. Luckily for Pluto, the pepper makes the clam sneeze, freeing it from Pluto's mouth. This short has the distinction of being not only Mickey and Pluto's last together, but also the last short in the Mickey Mouse theatrical cartoon series.

Mickey and Pluto's time together in shorts may have been over, but Pluto's time on television was not. In 1954, Walt Disney launched a new television show called *Disneyland*. One of the functions of the show was to help fund the development of his family-oriented theme park of the same name. Each episode of the show represented tales inspired by one of the sections of the new park. It was here that Disney showcased *Davy Crockett*, *20,000 Leagues Under the Sea*, and more. But Walt knew a star when he saw one, and the sixth episode of the show featured a segment called "A Story of Dogs," a tribute to Mickey's pal and Walt's first canine star.

A year later, Walt launched what would become yet another groundbreaking television show. The *Mickey Mouse Club* was a variety show featuring song and dance numbers by a group of children and teenagers known as the Mouseketeers. Although largely focused on the young performers, each episode also featured Mickey Mouse shorts. As fate would have it, the 1949 short *Pueblo Pluto* was the very first Mousekartoon that aired as part of the *Mickey Mouse Club*, heavily featuring Pluto in a story about trying to hide his bone in a cactus patch from a young pup who wants to take it from him.

In 1990, Pluto made a return to film with a role in the animated featurette *The Prince and the Pauper*—released along with *The Rescuers Down Under*—in which he plays Mickey's faithful companion. In 1999, Pluto again appeared as Mickey's faithful pet in a retelling of "The Gift of the Magi," one of three segments in *Mickey's Once Upon a Christmas*. This was followed up by a turn in *Mickey's Twice Upon a Christmas*, in which Pluto gets in a fight with Mickey and runs away. Pluto ends up on a train to the North Pole where he meets and befriends Santa Claus. Pluto also appears in 2004's *Mickey, Donald, and Goofy: The Three Musketeers*.

In 2013, the Disney Channel premiered a series of brand-new shorts. Drawing inspiration from the *Mickey Mouse* shorts of the 1930s, the new series has received critical acclaim and won multiple Emmy Awards. And at the center of the shorts is none other than Mickey's pal Pluto, who appears in *Space Walkies*, in which Pluto and Mickey travel to outer space; *Doggone Biscuits*, in which Minnie accidentally overfeeds Pluto and must figure out how to make him lose the weight he's gained before Mickey finds out what she's done; and *Coned*, in which Mickey, determined to show Pluto that wearing a dog cone is not so bad, puts one on himself. Unfortunately, Mickey is unable to see where he is going and ends up putting himself in danger, from which Pluto must rescue him.

Whether he has been on television or not, Pluto has remained a constant figure at the Disney Parks since they opened. In fact, he is one of the most commonly sighted characters at the Parks. The playful pup can usually be found greeting guests at Walt Disney World® Resort, and has even been known to join diners at Disney hotels and restaurants. But, fittingly, it is Disneyland where Pluto makes his true home, as he did on the *Disneyland* television show so many years ago. It is here that Pluto's doghouse can be found, as part of Mickey's Toontown. He has also been immortalized in a bronze statue prominently located outside of Sleeping Beauty Castle, where he can be seen by all guests entering the Park as a reminder of Pluto's prominent role in Mickey's—and Walt Disney's—success.

MAKE IT YOUR OWN

One of the great things about IncrediBuilds™ models is that each one is completely customizable. The untreated, natural wood can be decorated with paints, pencils, pens, beads, sequins—the list goes on and on!

Before you start building and decorating your model, read through the included instruction sheet so you understand how all the pieces come together. Then choose a theme—a replica of the original, or something completely different? The possibilities are endless! Here are some sample projects to get your creative juices flowing.

> It's best to paint your model once it's fully assembled.

Pluto Replica

Create your own version of Mickey's faithful friend with these simple instructions.

WHAT YOU NEED:
- Paints (yellow, red, black, white, green, and light brown)
- Paintbrush

1. Paint the main body yellow.
2. Paint the ears, nose, and tail black.
3. Paint the eye areas white.
4. Paint the eyeballs black. Then add white highlights for the pupils.
5. Paint the tongue red.
6. Paint the collar green.
7. With a light brown, paint the smile lines and the lines on the front paws.
8. Add a highlight of white on the nose for a finishing touch.

Classic Cartoon

Try your hand at this vintage look from Pluto's past!

WHAT YOU NEED:

- Paint (black, white, and gray)
- Paintbrush

Tip: Experiment with mixing different amounts of white and black paint to create different shades of gray.

1. Paint the main body medium gray.

2. Paint the collar, ears, nose, and tail black.

3. Paint the eye areas a very light gray.

4. Paint the eyeballs black. Then add white highlights for the pupils.

5. Paint the mouth area around the tongue in black. Add a light gray highlight around the inner black line of the tongue.

6. Add thin black lines for the smile, the wrinkle above the nose, and the claws on the paws.

7. Add some freckles and whiskers on the muzzle with black paint.

GOOD BOY!

Like every dog in the world, Pluto loves a good bone to chew on! Show Pluto what a good dog he is by painting all the bones he could ever want.

A Division of Insight Editions
PO Box 3088
San Rafael, CA 94912
www.insighteditions.com
www.incredibuilds.com

 Find us on Facebook: www.facebook.com/InsightEditions
 Follow us on Twitter: @insighteditions

Library of Congress Cataloging-in-Publication Data available.

ISBN: 978-1-68298-199-3

Publisher: Raoul Goff
Associate Publisher: Jon Goodspeed
Art Director: Chrissy Kwasnik
Designer: Evelyn Furuta and Lauren Chang
Project Editors: Erum Khan and Holly Fisher
Editorial Assistant: Kaia Waller
Production Editor: Lauren LePera
Associate Production Manager: Sam Taylor
Product Development Manager: Rebekah Piatte
Model Designer: Kat Tang, TeamGreen

ROOTS of PEACE   REPLANTED PAPER

Insight Editions, in association with Roots of Peace, will plant two trees for each tree used in the manufacturing of this book. Roots of Peace is an internationally renowned humanitarian organization dedicated to eradicating land mines worldwide and converting war-torn lands into productive farms and wildlife habitats. Roots of Peace will plant two million fruit and nut trees in Afghanistan and provide farmers there with the skills and support necessary for sustainable land use.

Manufactured in China

10 9 8 7 6 5 4 3 2 1

ABOUT THE AUTHOR

Eden Greenberg lives in Connecticut with her husband, dog, and two cats. She is an avid reader and loves to cook.

Photo Credit
Page 27:
enchanted_fairy/shutterstock.com (top);
Lucy Clark/dreamstime.com (bottom)